THIS is NOT a Bedtime STORY

BY WILL MABBITT

& FRED BLUNT

PUFFIN

It was Sophie's bedtime . . .

So Sophie's dad began to read . . .

Today is a very special day.

Today is Pink Kitten's . . .

Birthday!

Yay!

Princess Pink Kitten
is having a
Birthday Picnic.

It's *always* Pink
Kitten's birthday,

said Sophie.

Here come
Pink Kitten's friends,
Barney, Lulu and
Squeaker.

yoohoo!

Pink Kitten might
eat that mouse,

said Sophie.

NOT in *this* story, Sophie
– Squeaker's her friend!

I wish she'd invited a LION, said Sophie.

Er ... OK, said Dad.

It's time for Princess Pink Kitten and her friends to play some party games!

Yay!

Yay!

Lulu has given Pink Kitten
a birthday present!

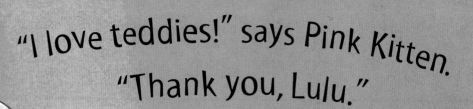

"I love teddies!" says Pink Kitten.
"Thank you, Lulu."

I bet she wished she had
been given a *lightsabre!*

said Sophie.

A *lightsabre?*
Why would Pink Kitten
want a *lightsabre?*

He's been gotten by a
Robot Dinosaur!

said Sophie.

They will if they use Pink Kitten's CAR!

said Sophie.

STOMP

Uh, oh ... WATCH OUT!
Pink Kitten, he's coming back!!!
Quick – fire rockets!!

cried Sophie.

AAAARGH!

Pink Kitten's car has
a *rocket launcher*?!

asked Dad.

Of course not,
silly ...

SCR

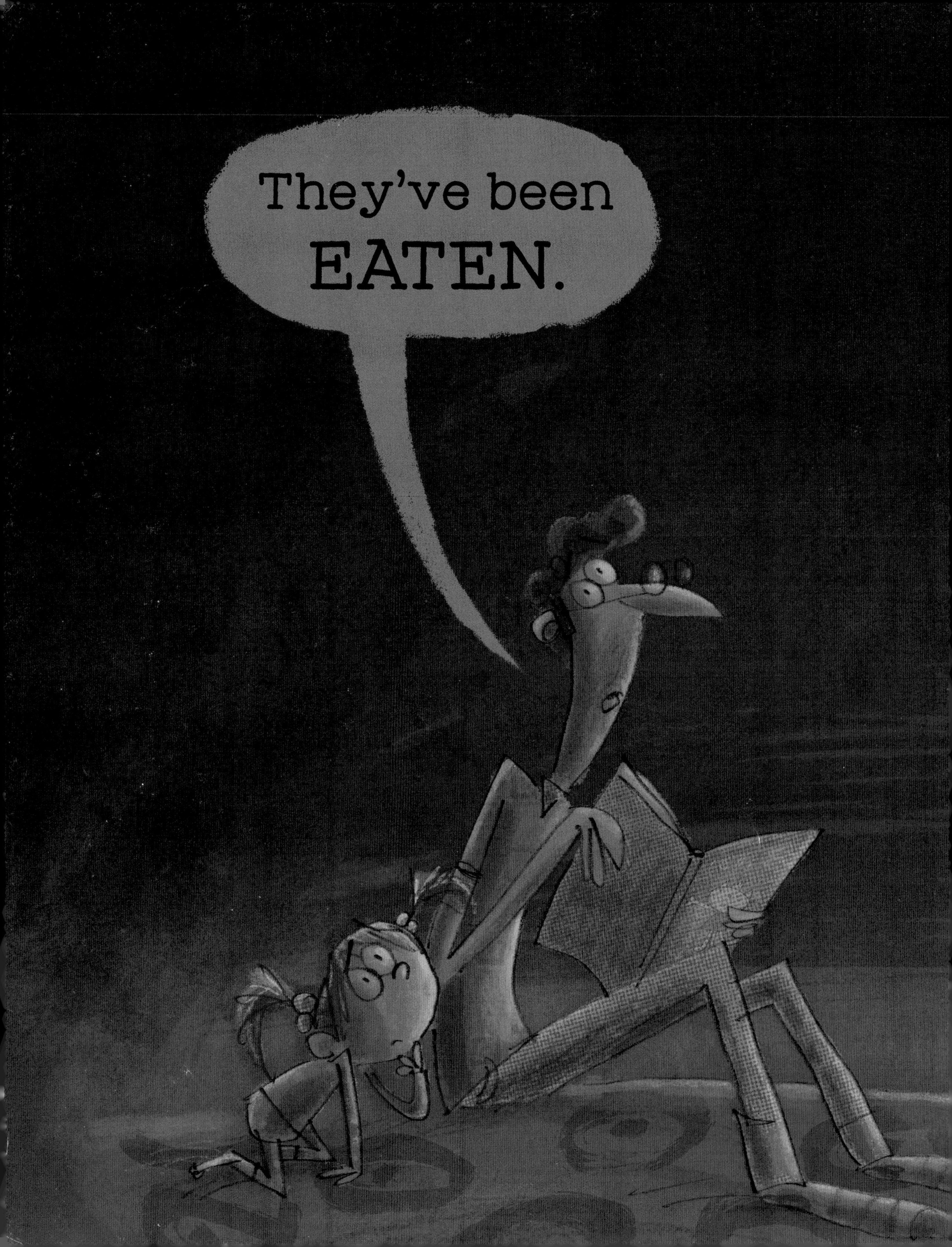
They've been EATEN.

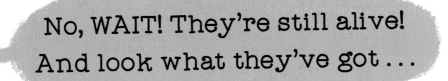

No, WAIT! They're still alive!
And look what they've got . . .

shouted Sophie.

Whoosh

Crash

CRASH

HOORAY
for Pink Kitten!
She's rescued Barney!

Pink Kitten yawned.
It was time to go home.
It had, after all, been...

A VERY exciting

yawn

It had, after all, been
a VERY exciting day.

To Hannah – W. M.

For Bonnie, my real-life Sophie – F. B.

PUFFIN BOOKS

UK | USA | Canada | Ireland | Australia | India | New Zealand | South Africa

Puffin Books is part of the Penguin Random House group of companies
whose addresses can be found at global.penguinrandomhouse.com.

puffinbooks.com

First published 2016

001

Printed in China

A CIP catalogue record for this book is available from the British Library

ISBN: 978–0–141–35738–6